Pennyweather's Proprietary Potion

Written by Arthur Conway
Illustrated by Dennis Juan Ma

Contents

NELSON
CENGAGE Learning™
For learning solutions, visit **cengage.com.au**

Meet the Characters

Arthur Conway

A boy from the village of Croaker.

Phineas Pennyweather

A travelling salesman.

Uncle Amos

Arthur's uncle.

Mrs Conway

Arthur's mother.

The villagers

Croaker's inhabitants.

Dear Reader

For those of you who wish to know how I became a successful and respected millionaire, here is my authorised biography. Almost all of it is true, except for the bits that aren't. I hope my story serves as an inspiration for all who believe you can get rich without working hard. That, of course, might be one of the bits that isn't true. That's for you to decide!

Arthur Conway
Author

Croaker

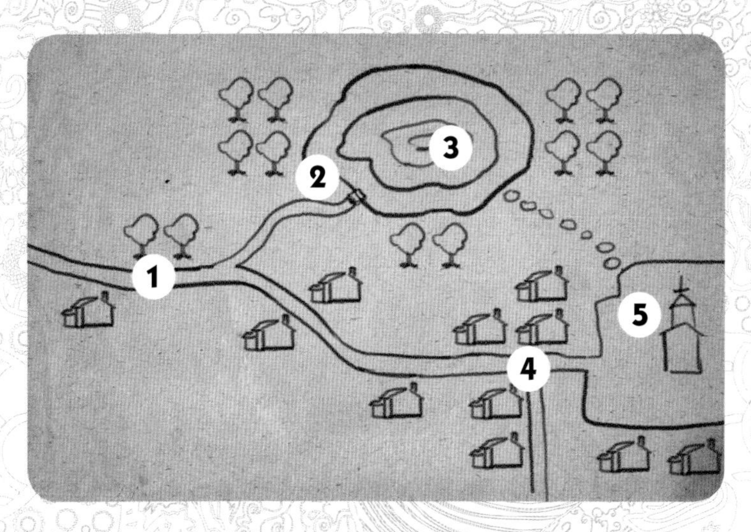

1. The road to the village
2. The jetty
3. The pond
4. The village of Croaker
5. The church

1 At the Village Pond

How did it all start? It was the first Saturday of summer, as I recall. The entire population of Croaker under the age of thirteen gathered around the village pond. The braver of us sat with their legs dangling off the jetty at the village pond. Dotted around the banks, the squeamish gathered in groups, at a safe distance, out of range of mischievously flung maggots or stinking strips of bacon that had, until that morning, been hidden in jars under beds until they'd turned green.

As a member of the brave group, I was on the jetty. Each time one of us threaded a wriggling maggot or a slimy strip of green bacon onto our hook, a chorus of "eergh, yuck" would arise from around the pond. Spurred on by the murmurs of disgust, we maggot impalers and bacon threaders would stand, basking in the revulsion that we imagined was thinly disguised admiration at our bravery. Studiously avoiding any glance at the onlookers, we would toss our baited lines into the murky pond, and resume our seats.

It had been barely five minutes since the commencement of Croaker's seasonal eel fishing spectacle when the first catch was hauled out of the pond, causing a commotion both on and off the jetty. After due examination, the writhing eel was placed in a wicker basket, slimy hands were wiped on shirts and trousers, and the proud angler embarked upon a tour of display.

The mixture of curiosity and horror the eel provoked amongst the anglers and onlookers was so strong that none of us noticed the horse and cart trundling down the rough, earthen road towards the village. Those of us on the jetty, disappointed that we had been denied the glory of the first catch of the season, stared resolutely at the surface of the pond,

willing an even bigger and slimier eel to swallow our bait and restore our pride.

"Good morning!" boomed a voice, startling all of us. Along with a dozen other pairs of eyes, I looked towards the man who had spoken. He was sitting atop his cart, tipping a top hat towards us.

"Phineas Pennyweather, purveyor of proprietary potions," he announced, sweeping a hand towards the lettering along the side of his brightly coloured cart, as if to confirm his identity. We stared at the stranger in silence, each of us wondering what a purveyor of proprietary potions was. It sounded serious. I'm sure I wasn't the only one who suspected we were about to get into trouble for some unknown indiscretion that involved maggots, green bacon, ponds or eels.

"Can you tell me the name of this village?" continued the stranger. "I fear I have taken a wrong turning."

"Croaker," I replied.

"I beg your pardon?" said the man, mistaking my answer for an insult. "Impudent scallywag!" He drew a small, square bottle out of his coat pocket and took a theatrical swig. He cleared his throat. "Very well, I shall ask once more, this time without croaking."

"No, sir," I explained. "The village. It's called Croaker."

"Ah," said the man. "Well, we shall have to see about fixing that. What's your name, young lad?"

"Conway, sir," I replied. "My name is Arthur Conway."

The man replaced his top hat and, with a nod towards me, twitched his horse's reins. "Good day, Arthur Conway."

A few moments later, the stranger and his horse and cart disappeared around a bend in the road. Curious as we were, we had other more immediate jobs to finish. We returned to the task of clearing the pond of eels and upsetting the onlookers. Alas, the groundwork for that job had already been laid while our attention was elsewhere.

"Where's my eel?" came an accusatory shout. The boy who'd captured the first eel and the morning's glory held an empty wicker basket aloft. "It's escaped."

It took less than thirty seconds for the squeamish amongst the under-thirteen

population of Croaker to flee noisily towards the village. The prospect of an unseen and highly disgruntled eel wriggling through the grass surrounding the pond made sure of that. And, without an audience, there seemed little point in the brave group staying either. Of course, none of us wanted to admit that, so it took a few minutes of glumly staring at the ripples on the pond before I thought of an option for retreat that would maintain our pride.

"Let's go and see what that Phineas Pennyweather's doing," I suggested.

"Right-o, Arthur," agreed a chorus of relieved voices at once. We packed up, and less than two minutes later, the village pond was deserted, save for a solitary eel wriggling towards its muddy brown waters.

2 Phineas Pennyweather

By the time we arrived at the village square, Croaker was anything but deserted. As I led the way into the square, Phineas Pennyweather was erecting a large canvas banner on his cart. At the same time, he was also declaring to anyone within hearing distance that no matter what ailed them, the cure to the villagers' problems was at hand. The rarity of strangers visiting our village would have been enough to attract attention when he creaked to a halt in the square. His banner and his booming announcement guaranteed it.

"Malaise, ill-health, minor irritations and plagues of the mind and body are all around us, lurking inside our bodies, lurking in the soil, the water, our very

Pennyweather's
Proprietary Potion
Phineas Pennyweather

food, waiting to erupt into life-threatening disease and crippling discomfort!" announced Pennyweather gravely to the crowd of onlookers. The villagers, who had, until that moment, been blithely unaware of the lurking dangers of life, muttered amongst each other.

Pennyweather opened a wooden box and held aloft a small, square bottle, just like the one he had drunk from earlier. "But never fear, good citizens of Croaker! At last, I, Phineas Pennyweather, bring you relief. In this small bottle I have distilled years of scientific research and the marvels of modern medicine." He uncorked the bottle and took a deep, melodramatic sniff of its contents. "Pennyweather's Proprietary Potion," he beamed, with the proud yet humble confidence of a man who had single-handedly defeated every bodily complaint.

I wondered who would be the first to put up their hand. Eventually, my Uncle Amos did. He had shuffled out of the butcher's shop with half a dozen rashers of bacon to replace those that had mysteriously disappeared a fortnight ago from my Aunty Enid's cupboard.

"What does it cure?" he asked.

"What ails you?" inquired Phineas Pennyweather.

"Well, I do have a sore back," admitted Uncle Amos. "Although I don't think it's caused by anything lurking there."

"A sore back!" repeated Phineas Pennyweather in amazement. "Good sir, that is exactly the kind of ailment my proprietary potion will alleviate. To think that you should happen to be in this village square at exactly this moment! It's altogether too much of a coincidence."

"Well, I was just getting some bacon," began Uncle Amos, before being silenced by Phineas Pennyweather.

"Nonsense, my good man. It is fate. And because fate has brought us together in such a timely fashion, I shall bow to its wishes and award you this first bottle of Pennyweather's Proprietary Potion absolutely free."

I watched as all the villagers, astounded at Uncle Amos's good fortune, burst into spontaneous applause. I was tempted to reveal my part in starting the chain of bacon-related events that led Uncle Amos towards his meeting with fate, but decided to hold my tongue. There was no telling whether Pennyweather's Proprietary Potion would cure Aunty Enid's annoyance at discovering who'd commandeered her bacon.

Seconds after a beaming Uncle Amos received his small, square bottle, along with whispered instructions as to how to apply it, another voice cried out: "What about grumpiness and melancholy?" It was old Widow Parker's neighbour, who was standing next to the woman herself. Old Widow Parker was scowling at her neighbour even more than usual. I'd never seen her smile – not even when I'd won the county cricket match by hitting a mighty "six" through her window. Not only was it a magnificent shot, but I'd offered to pay for the window with my very own pocket money. Surely nothing would cheer her up!

Phineas Pennyweather's face lit up. "Incredible," he breathed, looking skywards and shaking his head. "I was just about to ask about that specific complaint!"

He followed the neighbour's nervous sideways glance and addressed old Widow Parker. "Madam, Pennyweather's Proprietary Potion will once more put a skip in your step and a smile on your face. Now I am convinced beyond all doubt that fate indeed led me to this merry village, and if I hadn't already given away a bottle of my potion, you'd be getting one for free."

Widow Parker looked about as optimistic as I'd seen her in years.

"So how much would you expect to pay for happiness and contentment?" continued Pennyweather. "Ten pounds? Five pounds? No, ladies and gentlemen, a mere fraction of that is all I ask. Five shillings a bottle, and my real reward will be in knowing that I shall leave this dear lady in better shape than I found her."

Evidently, that was a fair price for skipping and smiling, and if Widow Parker hadn't dug into her bag and brought out five shillings, I'm sure at least five people in the crowd would have chipped in a shilling each to remove the permanent frown from her face.

"I've had an upset tummy for years," called out the village vicar, Dr Boodlethwaite, accompanied by much nodding amongst the crowd. Every Sunday they'd had to strain their ears to hear the vicar's service over the gurgling coming from the pulpit. "Will it cure that?"

"Reverend, your prayers are answered," replied Phineas Pennyweather. "My proprietary potion will clean your insides out with such explosive force that all troublesome digestive problems will be expelled once and for all."

As soon as I heard that, nothing was going to stop me being in the front pew come tomorrow. I just hoped the potion could contain itself until the morning, because that was a cure I just had to see.

Sore elbows. Headaches. Anxiety attacks. Indigestion. Overeating. Undereating. Baldness. Excessive hairiness. It seemed the entire village had been suffering in silence, plagued by a plethora of maladies, all of which could be simply and effectively cured by the appropriate application of Pennyweather's Proprietary Potion, either internally or externally. The first Saturday of summer brought not only relief from Croaker's long winter and cool spring, but also a long list of discontentments felt by its inhabitants.

I had no idea things were so bad. I couldn't believe I hadn't noticed how ill everybody was. I wondered if Pennyweather's Proprietary Potion would help me to concentrate better.

3 The Proprietary Potion

By noon, an entire case of small, square bottles had been sold and dispensed to the long-suffering residents of Croaker. Not a moment too soon, I reflected, as I wandered home. Our entire village had narrowly avoided total extinction.

"Catch anything, Arthur?" enquired my mother, as I flopped down in a kitchen chair.

"Thankfully not," I replied, thinking she meant one of the dozens of severe illnesses that were lurking inside, outside and around the villagers. "But being around all those invalids has made me feel a little weak." It was true. Now that the full extent of the epidemics sweeping Croaker

had been revealed, I was worried that I too might have been infected with something dreadful. I was pretty sure I felt the faintest murmurings of a headache, and somehow, my tummy didn't feel quite like it should have. I wondered if my heart was beating too fast. Or was it too slow?

"What on earth are you talking about?" asked my mother, frowning. I told her about Phineas Pennyweather and his fortunate appearance, just in the nick of time.

"Hmm," she said, once she'd heard my account of the morning's events. "I think I'd better go and talk to Uncle Amos. He can get a bit carried away."

"He's lucky he didn't get carried away," I observed. "On a stretcher."

Mum gave a non-committal harrumph.

"That doesn't sound too good either," I said. "Sounds like something's irritating your throat. It's a shame Pennyweather has sold out of his proprietary potion. That might have helped."

"You're right," nodded my mother. "Something is irritating me. But I don't think Pennyweather's Proprietary Potion will help." She wiped her hands on a tea towel and headed for the door. "I'll be at Amos and Enid's if anybody needs me."

I was left alone, looking glumly at the tea towel. There was no telling what disturbing bugs it now harboured. I considered making a sandwich, but the thought of having to first find my magnifying glass and examine every lettuce leaf for lurking microbes was exhausting. I decided I'd rather see what

effect Pennyweather's Proprietary Potion was having on Uncle Amos. I rushed out the door and ran along the path to catch up with my mother.

"It works a treat, Maggie," said Amos brightly when my mother questioned him about the potion he'd been given. "Look!" He bent down and touched his toes, which was something we hadn't seen Uncle Amos do for years.

"We just followed Mr Pennyweather's advice," added Aunty Enid. She handed her sister-in-law a scrap of paper, on which Uncle Amos had scrawled the instructions

Pennyweather had whispered to him, just in case he caught amnesia before he made it home.

My mother looked sceptically at the scribbled instructions. "Lie flat on a hard floor for one hour. Roll over and ask a trained physician or spouse, whoever is handiest, to gently rub the proprietary potion into your back for one more hour. Rest for a further twenty minutes. Avoid heavy lifting or exertion thereafter."

"It's magic," winked Uncle Amos.

"It's nonsense," retorted my mother. "You've had a lie-down, a back rub and a rest. No wonder you feel better. Pennyweather's Proprietary Potion has had nothing to do with it!"

Uncle Amos shook his head and gave his sister a condescending smile. "No, no, Maggie. It works a treat. You just have to *believe* in it."

My mother rolled her eyes and sighed.

"You seem a little uptight, dear," offered Aunty Enid. "Mr Pennyweather told Amos that his potion also helps relieve stress. Exactly the same procedure. Would you like to try some?"

I thought that was an excellent idea worth trying. Unfortunately, my mother declined.

By nightfall, almost all of Croaker was happily convinced of the potion's efficacy. Throughout the village, people hastened their salvation by rubbing

Pennyweather's Proprietary Potion in carefully measured circles and supping it in carefully measured teaspoons. I say "almost" because my mother remained unconvinced. She came home that evening muttering "charlatan", which I supposed meant some kind of doctor, like "paediatrician" or "dermatologist".

I couldn't worry myself about it too much anyway. I had to rest. I was certain I was coming down with a fever. After my mother and I returned from Uncle Amos and Aunty Enid's house, I'd consulted the little black book of household ailments that was kept in the bathroom cabinet. I was alarmed to find I had most of the symptoms of bubonic plague. Luckily, I'd diagnosed it early enough that I might still survive. I resolved to run down to the village square first thing in the morning, before Pennyweather packed up and left, to get my own small, square bottle of potion. That, and the thought of watching the vicar explode during tomorrow's service, kept me clinging to life through the dark hours before dawn.

4 A Business Proposition

The next morning, before the sun rose, I was already padding my way silently downstairs. One of the side effects of bubonic plague that hadn't been mentioned in the little black book of household ailments was insomnia. When I felt better, I thought, I'd write to the author and tell her to update that chapter.

I left the house and made my way through the darkness to the village square, where I was relieved to see Pennyweather's horse and cart where they had been left yesterday. The horse was slumbering, and there was no sign of life beneath the tarpaulins and blankets in the cart. I was about to climb up and rummage through its contents in search of Phineas

Pennyweather and a cure for the plague when I heard a wail and a splash.

I whirled around. The sound came from the village pond. Forgetting my own impending death for a moment, I ran out of the square and down the path that led to the jetty.

"Eergh!" came a voice, which I recognised as Pennyweather's. I raced onto the jetty, just in time to see Phineas Pennyweather standing, soaking wet, in the middle of the murky pond water. He'd clearly slipped and fallen in.

"Are you OK?" I asked breathlessly, as I made it to the planks of the jetty.

"Arthur Conway! What are you doing here?" he spluttered, coughing the last of Croaker's pond out of his lungs.

"I came down to get some of your proprietary potion," I explained.

I was about to tell Pennyweather about the urgency of my predicament when I noticed something beside his dripping body: a row of small, square, half-empty bottles. "Why are you tipping your proprietary potion into the pond?" I gasped.

"I ... er ... umm," mumbled Pennyweather in an embarrassed tone.

"Hang on!" I said, the truth of the situation dawning on me. "You're not tipping it into the pond! You're doing the opposite. The bottles are half-full, not half-empty." I stared at Phineas Pennyweather in disbelief. He stared at me. I didn't know what to say. Fortunately, he broke the silence between us.

"Eergh!" he cried. A writhing movement in his trouser leg caught my eye, and I watched in horror as an eel's

head emerged between his cuff and his sock. As any self-respecting under-thirteen-year old Croaker boy would, I seized the slimy creature and pulled it out of Pennyweather's trousers, holding it aloft.

"Congratulations, Mr Conway," coughed Pennyweather, recovering his composure. He sat upright and stared at the wriggling eel. "The first catch of the day."

I looked around the deserted banks of the pond, slowly becoming lighter as the dawn approached. "Not much point when there's no audience," I muttered.

"I know exactly how you feel," agreed Pennyweather. "Now, listen carefully, young fellow. You've caught me in, shall we say, an awkward position. But there's no need to inflame the situation. I like to think of myself as a purveyor of hope and optimism, you see. Think of how these expectations would be cruelly dashed if the villagers ever learned of our ... our ... business meeting. Yes, that's right, young man. I have a business proposition for you."

And so it was that, as the sun rose over the village of Croaker, I joined the esteemed ranks of the medical profession. In all the excitement, I quite forgot about my fatal condition and it was only later that day I remembered I had bubonic plague. Luckily, it had seemed to cure itself, which was quite contrary to what the little black book of household ailments and their remedies considered were the normal sequence of events. I resolved to add that little snippet too, when I wrote to the author with my helpful update.

As the villagers of Croaker filed into church later that morning, the atmosphere of hopefulness and optimism was almost tangible. Uncle Amos, who had undergone another two-hour-and-twenty-minute round of treatment after breakfast, skipped up the stone steps. Widow Parker smiled and nodded at the other villagers, which was as big a miracle as any that had occurred in our stone church's 500-year existence. Girls compared notes about how freckles had grown fainter before their very eyes and how, within another month, they quite expected them to disappear altogether. Bald men lowered their crowns so admiring neighbours could see for themselves how much fuller their remaining locks appeared. Overweight ladies declared with pride that, after a healthy dose of Pennyweather's Proprietary Potion, they hadn't felt like eating a thing. Quite the opposite in fact.

At ten o'clock, the congregation fell silent and strained their ears for the slightest gurgle as Dr Boodlethwaite walked, somewhat stiffly, to the pulpit. His normally ruddy complexion had been replaced by a frighteningly pallid demeanour and a look of slight alarm. My heart sank as I realised that his troublesome digestive problems had already been expelled once and for all. I was disappointed. Much to my mother's

surprise, I'd put my name down for the working bee that cleaned the church after the service. I'd hoped to be kept busy peeling bits of the vicar off the church walls, but it looked like my morning was going to be a lot duller now.

"Welcome to you all," began Dr Boodlethwaite. "I'd like to begin this morning's service by ..."

A searing, wheezing groan erupted from beneath the vicar's cassock and reverberated around the congregation. The vicar's jaw dropped, along with those of most of the villagers gathered in the church.

Barely five minutes later, we were all outside the church, shaking each other's hands and bidding our farewells and Sunday-best wishes. I was delighted to

discover that Pennyweather's Proprietary Potion possessed not only a plethora of medical benefits – it had also given us the shortest service on record.

As his new business partner since dawn that morning, I knew that Phineas Pennyweather and I were onto something. If the reaction of the villagers of Croaker was anything to go by, the future was indeed bright for bottled hope, optimism and pond water.

5 Arthur Conway Returns

Ten years passed by after that fateful Saturday morning when I'd sat with my legs dangling off the jetty at the village pond. On the rare occasions when I did return home to Croaker, I no longer indulged in leg-dangling, of course. Instead, I strolled through the quiet little village, swinging my silver cane and adjusting my top hat to just the right angle of jauntiness befitting a millionaire.

"Arthur, are you coming back to settle down in Croaker? There's plenty of eels still left in the pond," called one of my old fishing companions.

"Alas," I replied, "my eeling days are over. Instead I must dedicate my life to the demanding career of a medical professional."

That wasn't strictly true, of course. A slight disagreement a few years ago with some lawyers, a magistrate and an Act of Parliament meant that my dear friend Phineas and I were no longer technically allowed to call ourselves "medical professionals". Astonishingly, the judges and lawmakers had decided we couldn't even claim that our proprietary potion had any medical benefits whatsoever. It hadn't affected our business a jot. Pennyweather and Conway's Proprietary Potion continued to demonstrate exactly the same effects as it had previously, and sales continued to soar.

Shortly after that, more lawyers, another magistrate and a further Act of Parliament thought they could undermine hardworking ex-medical professionals by forcing us to put a list of ingredients on our small, square bottles.

"Water, flavouring," we wrote, which was perfectly true, and sales continued to skyrocket. It seemed that no one needed to know exactly what the flavouring was, which was a relief because I had no idea myself. Who knew what lurked in the deepest, darkest recesses of village ponds?

I just wished the lawyers, magistrates and parliamentarians had actually tried some of our proprietary potion. They did seem a little uptight, and as legions of our loyal customers had attested, our potion also helped to relieve stress. I was almost sure it hadn't done anyone any harm.

It was a hot summer's day, and I wandered up the path to the jetty where it had all begun. I was delighted to see that even though a decade had passed, a new crop of under-thirteen-year olds were still enjoying adventures around the village pond. Half were still huddled in groups, periodically voicing their disgust at the activities of the other half, who were still happily hunting eels. One of the boys had one of the new-fangled bottles of lemonade, which, as the current craze dictated, had been carbonated. They were passing the bottle from one to another, slurping the fizzy liquid greedily.

"Perhaps we should diversify into thirst-quenching drinks to refresh youngsters," I mused as I watched the children play. "We could use the same brown "flavouring", and just add sugar and bubbles." I made a mental note to suggest that to Phineas when I returned to our factory in the city. We could call it "Croaker Cooler". On hot summer days, it would sell like crazy.

I turned and headed back to the village. I was glad to see that some things never changed. As an ex-Croaker resident, I hadn't changed much either. Of course, I had finer clothes, a half-share in a proprietary potion empire, and I lived in a magnificent mansion in the heart of the city. But, like the under-thirteen-year old Croaker boy I'd once been, I still kept jars of green stuff hidden under my bed.

I still felt a twinge of guilt every time I came home, however. My mother still disapproved of my illustrious career and, no matter how often I pointed out that "charlatan" was not an approved medical term, she still shook her head and muttered it whenever I visited.

A dose of hope and optimism, courtesy of Pennyweather and Conway's Proprietary Potion, would help that – Mother's disapproval, not my twinges of guilt.

I didn't need a swig from a small square bottle for any such feelings. I told myself the green stuff hidden under my bed worked just as well as a proprietary potion. It wasn't old rotting bacon, you see. It came from banks, folded nicely into your pockets and, as long as you believed it made you feel better, I found it to be an excellent remedy for keeping the feelings of guilt at bay.